Thor
and the
Master of Magic

by

Kevin Crossley-Holland

Illustrated by Siku

First published in 2007 in Great Britain by
Barrington Stoke Ltd
18 Walker St, Edinburgh, EH3 7LP

www.barringtonstoke.co.uk

ISBN: 978-1-84299-478-8

Printed in Great Britain by Bell & Bain Ltd

Contents

1   Between Worlds   1

2   Somewhere to Sleep   10

3   Three Wallops   19

4   In the Hall of the Giant-King   27

5   Running Races   37

6   A Drop to Drink   42

7   Lifting and Wrestling   48

8   Master of Magic   57

   Battle Cards   64

Chapter 1

Between Worlds

"Giants," growled the god Thor. "I like nothing so much as a good fight with a giant. I'll wallop the Giant-King with my hammer."

Thor's friend Loki smiled a twisted smile. Loki was a trickster. "You'll never wallop the Giant-King," he said. "You won't even lay a finger on him."

Thor snorted. "I've got to fight the giants," he said. "If I don't, they'll attack us. They'll take over our kingdom. Remember my magic hammer. I can fight the giants with that." Thor checked that his hammer was tied fast to his belt, and then he stepped into his chariot.

Loki's eyes flickered like little orange flames. "The Giant-King," he said, "is a master of magic."

Thor grabbed the chariot's silver reins. "Well!" he boomed. "Are you coming, or not?"

Loki climbed up into the chariot. "I'll come for the ride," he said. "And I'll come and see what games the Giant-King plays with you, Mighty Thor!"

Thor roared. The two goats that pulled his chariot jumped forward, and the wheels made the sound of thunder. Loki fell backward into his seat. It was thickly padded with reindeer skins.

****

Sunrise.

Thor and Loki rode past the glossy, marble palaces of the gods and goddesses. They galloped over a great plain criss-crossed with shining, silky spiders' webs.

Then Thor and Loki left Asgard, kingdom of the gods. Slowly they picked their way across a shimmering rainbow bridge.

The watchman-god saw them leave and blew a long, sad blast on his horn. Everyone heard it. All the gods and goddesses. Each human being and elf and dwarf and giant. Far down in the Underworld, all the rotting creatures and monsters heard it, even the dead.

Thor and Loki came down to Middle Earth, home of human beings and elves and dwarfs and giants. All day they rode across grim and gritty fields of lava. Just before dark they came to a green valley with a little, low farmhouse snug in the middle of it. The farmhouse looked as if it was growing out of the ground because it had a grassy roof.

The farmer and his wife knew who Thor and Loki were. They shouted out for their son and daughter, Rapid and Ristil. They began to shake.

"You've nothing to fear," Thor told them. "All we want is a hot meal."

"And somewhere to sleep," added Loki.

"We'll give you what we have, but we have very little," the farmer said.

Loki sniffed.

"A couple of chickens will do," said Thor.

The farmer's wife shook her head. "We have no meat."

"No meat!" bellowed Thor.

The farmer and his wife put their hands over their eyes. So did Rapid. But his little sister Ristil put her hands on her hips.

"No meat at all!" she repeated. "Not even a pig's trotter. Not even a lamb's ear."

"No meat," Thor said again. "Well, we'll eat my two goats then."

Thor killed the goats, the farmer's wife skinned them, the farmer chopped them up, and Rapid and Ristil skewered the meat and roasted it on the fire.

Thor laid out the two skins by the fire.

"Eat all the meat," he told the farmer and his family, "but be very careful with the bones. Throw each and every one down on to these two skins."

But Rapid was only 11 years old. He hadn't eaten any meat for weeks, not even an old rabbit. He was so hungry that he split open one of the goat's bones and sucked the rich marrow-juice out of it. Then he threw the bone down on to one of the skins.

At dawn, while everyone was still asleep, Thor lifted his hammer over the bones and skins of his two goats. He blessed them. The goats got to their feet and began to bleat. Then Thor noticed one of them was limping.

The god yelped, and the farmer and his family all jumped out of bed. Loki opened one eye.

"I told you to be careful," Thor growled. "Who cracked one of this goat's bones? Who was it?"

The woman gulped. The two children hid their faces.

"Mercy!" the farmer begged. "Have mercy on us."

Thor grunted. "All right," he said. "I won't kill you, but I'll take Rapid and Ristil with me, as my servants."

"No," said Ristil.

"Yes," said Thor. "You can come with us to the fortress of the Giant-King."

Chapter 2
Somewhere to Sleep

Thor the giant-killer left his two goats and his chariot with the farmer and his wife.

He filled his sack with the meat left over from last night's supper and then he and Loki and their two servants, Rapid and Ristil, set off. They walked a long way east. They walked until late afternoon. Then the kingdom of the giants rose up to meet them. They could see a row of jagged mountain peaks stretching right along the horizon.

The four travellers came down to the banks of a very wide, milky river. The icy water was hurling itself from rock to rock, spitting and snarling.

"On this side of the river we're safe," Loki told them. "On the other, we're not. This is the crossing-place."

"I've never been this far before," said Ristil.

"You'll be safe with me," Thor told her. "You and your brother."

"I wouldn't be so sure," Loki said.

There were some boats beached on the river bank. Thor told his servants to drag one down to the water, and then he took the oars and rowed them all across the angry river. The mountains rose up high above them.

"It's time for you to do some work," Loki told Rapid as soon as they'd crossed the river. "Scout around and find us somewhere cosy to sleep."

Thor grunted. "I give the orders here," he said. "Rapid, scout around and find us somewhere to sleep."

"Somewhere cosy," Loki added.

Rapid jumped out of the boat and ran towards a pine forest. Hours passed. It was dusk before he came running back.

"I've found an odd sort of hall," he announced. "It's standing in the middle of a forest clearing."

Over their heads, a screeching eagle flew round and round the four travellers.

"That eagle is watching us," Loki warned them.

"What for?" asked Ristil.

"Its supper," said Loki.

The four travellers picked their way through a gloomy pine forest until they came to the clearing. The eagle followed them.

"That's not a hall," said Loki, with a frown.

"What is it then?" asked Rapid.

"Look!" shouted Loki. "This front end is all open – from side to side and top to bottom. It's like a cave."

"Well," said Thor, "whatever it is, it's so big that I could put my own hall inside it."

"It'll keep the rain off our backs," said Rapid.

"And stop that eagle from pecking out our eyes," added Loki, "and gobbling up our guts."

Thor nodded. He turned to Loki. "In here," he said, "you can sleep easy."

"I never sleep easy," answered the Trickster.

When the four travellers had eaten half the meat in Thor's sack, they lay down. After their long trek, they soon fell fast asleep.

But at midnight, they were woken by low growling. They scrambled to their feet. The noise sounded as if it came from underground. No, it sounded as if the walls themselves were growling. It grew louder, much louder, and the ground began to sway and shake.

"An earth-quake!" shouted Thor. "Out! Everyone out!"

But at this moment, the growling stopped.

"Not an earth-quake," said Thor. He tugged his red beard.

"Everyone out," said Loki.

"I give the orders here," Thor said.

Little Ristil shivered. "We don't know what's outside," she said. "Why don't we go further in?"

"The girl's right," said Thor.

So the travellers held out their hands in front of them and slowly felt their way along the walls in the dark. Halfway down one wall, they came to another, much smaller room. It was even darker in here, and very stuffy.

"You three sleep in here," Thor told his friends. "I'll guard the door."

At dawn, Thor crept outside while everyone else was still asleep. There, in the clearing, he saw a sleeping giant.

Then the giant snorted and growled. And hearing him, Thor knew at once what the midnight noises had been.

Thor put his hand to the handle of his hammer, but then the giant opened one eye and stood up. He was much taller than any of the pine-trees.

"Who are you?" shouted Thor. "Who on earth are you?"

"I'm Big Bloke," bellowed the giant. "And I know who you are, all right. You're Thor." He pointed at Loki and Rapid and Ristil who had crept out of their cave-shelter and were standing looking at him. "And these little creatures," he went on, "they must be your three friends. Were you all sleeping in my glove?"

Then Big Bloke bent down and picked up his glove, his massive glove, open at one end. There was a small side-room for his thumb.

"What are you doing in our kingdom?" the giant boomed. "Small fry like you don't belong here."

"We're heading for the fortress of the Giant-King," Thor told him.

"Are you indeed?" said Big Bloke. "Well, I'll come along with you for a while. And I'll carry your sack. What do you say to that?"

But before Thor could say anything, the giant dropped Thor's sack into his own enormous bag, strapped it up, and strode away into the forest.

Chapter 3
Three Wallops

All day Big Bloke crashed his way through the forest. Not even Rapid could keep up with him. But in the blue hour before night fell, the giant began to sag. Then he slumped down under some pine trees.

"There are no houses or barns around here," Big Bloke told Thor. "Not even a glove! But these pine trees are as good as a roof. They'll keep you dry. Me, I'm done in. All I want to do is sleep."

Loki gave a sigh and the children flopped down. They were worn out.

"Help yourselves to my food," bellowed the giant. "If there's no meat left in your sack, eat some of mine." With that he yawned – his breath was as rotten as a rubbish tip – and then he rolled over.

"You two gather some wood and get a fire going," Thor told Rapid and Ristil. "I'll unstrap the bag and lay out all the meat."

But Thor, the strongest of all the gods, couldn't undo Big Bloke's sack – not a single strap. "They're made of metal," he told Loki.

"Or made with magic," grunted Loki. "The dwarfs once made a chain like that. Down in their dark caves, their eyes shone like glow-worms. They made a strong chain out of things that are not. They made it with the sound a cat makes when it moves, and a woman's beard, and the roots of a mountain and …"

"Shut up about the dwarfs!" growled Thor. "I'm starving."

Thor looked at Big Bloke, and the sprawling giant rolled over on to his back. His mouth flapped open and his breathing sounded like a flock of cawing crows. The thunder-god grabbed his hammer. He lifted it, and walloped the giant right in the middle of his fore-head.

Big Bloke opened one eye. "What was that?" he yawned. "Did a leaf just fall on my fore-head?"

Loki smiled a crooked smile. Thor said nothing.

"Have you had enough supper?" Big Bloke asked. "Why aren't you asleep yet?" But he didn't wait for Thor's reply. He just fell fast asleep again.

So Thor and his friends had to lie down without having eaten even a mouthful of food. But they couldn't sleep because they were so hungry. And now they had seen how Big Bloke's head was stronger than Thor's hammer, they were very scared too.

At midnight, Big Bloke started to snort and growl just as loudly as he had the night before. The springy floor of the pine forest shuddered and jumped, and all the birds living up in the trees flew away to somewhere more peaceful.

"I've had enough of this," Thor growled to himself. The god stood up, and crept over to Big Bloke. He grabbed his hammer, and cracked it – he walloped it – against the giant's skull.

Big Bloke sat up. "What was that?" he boomed. "Did an acorn fall on me?" The giant yawned. "Still awake, Thor? Still prowling around. What are you up to?"

"I can't sleep," growled Thor.

"Try again," the giant told him. "If at first you don't succeed ... you know what they say."

Thor backed away. He lay down next to his friends, but he still couldn't sleep.

Big Bloke's too big for me, he thought. *But I'll have one more go at him while he's asleep. And next time, I'll wallop him once and for all.*

Just before daybreak, Thor stretched and stood up again and sneaked over to Big Bloke. The giant was lying on his side. Thor grabbed his hammer, and swung it. He buried the whole head of the hammer in the giant's brains.

Big Bloke gave a long sigh and opened one eye. He rubbed his cheek. "Did a bird squit on me?" he muttered, still half-asleep.

Thor gazed at Big Bloke. Why didn't his magic hammer work any more? He couldn't work it out.

The giant sat up. "The fortress of the Giant-King is not far east from here," he boomed. "The giants there are much bigger than I am, and I tell you what. You keep your mouth shut. They won't stand for insults from tiddlers like you. They'll stuff your empty boasts back down your throat."

Thor felt furious. But what could he do?

"If I were you," said Big Bloke, "I'd go right back home." The giant stretched and stood up. He picked up his bag, and it still had

Thor's sack inside it. And then, without a single word, without so much as a backward look, Big Bloke stumped off into the gloomy pine forest towards the mountains.

Thor turned back to his three friends. "Wake up!" he roared. "Wake up!"

Chapter 4
In the Hall of the Giant-King

Thor and Loki and Rapid and Ristil hurried along a hill shaped like a saddle. Then they crossed three valleys. Three times they had to slither down steep ravines, and each one was deeper than the one before.

Faint with hunger, the travellers ran down onto a sandy plain. The Giant-King's fortress stood right in the middle of it, glinting in the sunlight.

Only when Thor and his friends had walked right up to the walls did they see just how high they were. Fifteen metres. Maybe even twenty metres. More than ten times as tall as Rapid and Ristil.

Thor grabbed the bars on the iron gates and shook them, but the gates were locked.

Loki looked at the gaps between the bars. "What about Rapid?" he said. "Rapid, you try."

"I give the orders here," said Thor. "You try, Rapid."

Rapid was slim. He had long arms and long legs. He slipped between two of the bars. Ristil was thin too. She followed him. Then Loki shoved his head between the bars.

"My head fits," he said. "So everything else will."

Then Thor tried to push his own head between the bars. It wouldn't fit.

"Big-head!" Loki laughed.

"Blabber-mouth!" growled Thor.

"Bumble-god!" Loki taunted him.

"You," grunted Thor. "You've always got a word for everything."

Thor was right, and that was why Loki's smile was so twisted. Long ago, the dwarfs had tried to sew his lips together to shut him up once and for all.

Thor grabbed two iron bars and pulled them just far enough apart to work his way between them.

Inside the gate, there was an enormous court-yard. All around were grim high halls, much larger than the glossy, marble palaces of the gods. The largest of them stood right in front of Thor and his friends. Its door was open.

What a sight! A bonfire made from tree trunks was blazing in the middle of the hall floor, and hundreds of giants, male giants and female giants and their giant children, were sitting on massive benches all along the walls. Did I say sitting? No. They were sprawling, they were lying and lolling and lazing, they were slurping and burping, arguing, guffawing, they were snorting and scratching themselves, they were poking and punching each other. The enormous, smoky hall was thick with their sweat and stink. It was loud with their booming shouts and the rasp and buzz of their heavy breathing.

One giant was sitting alone at the far end of the hall on a chair that was set up on a platform.

"That's the Giant-King," Thor said to himself. "Wallop!"

Then Thor led his friends up the hall between the rows of leering, jeering, sneering giants. "Greetings, King!" said Thor politely. After all, he was the guest and the king was his host.

The Giant-King ignored Thor.

"Greetings, I said!" Thor bellowed more loudly.

The Giant-King looked down his nose. "Who is this midget?" he asked. "This little imp? It can't be Thor. I must have made some mistake."

The thunder-god clenched and unclenched his fists. He kept his mouth shut.

"Well!" said the Giant-King. "I don't know. Maybe you're stronger than you look. Are you good at anything, or good for nothing? What can you and your friends do? No one's allowed to stay here without showing us some special skill."

"Let the little girl stay," drawled one young giant. He smiled at Ristil.

"She can stay," the Giant-King agreed. "She's as dainty as a daisy chain."

"I'm not!" protested Ristil.

"Well, Thor?" barked the Giant-King. "Don't know what to say, eh?"

Loki spoke up. "I have a skill, sir," he said, "and I'm ready to prove it. No giant in this hall can eat as fast as I can."

"Is that so?" said the Giant-King. "We'll soon see about that." He looked along the benches and pointed to a young giant. "Hey, you!" shouted the Giant-King. "Are you feeling hungry?"

"Always and always," bawled the young giant.

"All right. Come up here."

The Giant-King's servants carried a long table to the middle of the hall. They loaded it with necks of lamb and shoulders of pork and sides of ox and joints of mutton and pigs' trotters. There was meat covering the whole table – from one end to the other. Poor Thor and Rapid and Ristil! They were all so hungry that they couldn't even look at it.

Now the servants set down chairs for Loki and the young giant at each end of the table.

"Ready?" the Giant-King asked them. "Steady? Eat!"

All the giants in the hall got to their feet. They stamped and shouted and cheered.

Loki wolfed the meat, great hunks of it. So did the young giant. And as they ate, each of them moved his chair down along the table until they met right in the middle.

Loki had gobbled up every scrap of skin and flesh, and left nothing but bare bones. But the giant had eaten the bones and the wooden table as well.

Loki turned to Thor with a twisted smile. "I told you," he said. "A master of magic."

The Giant-King lifted up both hands and all the giants stopped shouting. They fell silent.

"I would say," he called out, "that Loki is the loser."

All the giants roared again. The walls of the Great Hall shuddered.

Chapter 5
Running Races

"So, Thor," scoffed the Giant-King. "What about this young lad? What can he do?"

Thor stared at Rapid and the boy shook his head. He combed his blond hair with his fingers. "Nothing special," Rapid muttered.

"That's not true," Ristil said. "You should see him run races."

"Very good," said the Giant-King. "But the slowest giant in this hall can beat the fastest man on Middle Earth. Believe me!"

The Giant-King led his visitors out of the hall into a field. A crowd of peering, leering, ambling, shambling giants came along behind them. The Giant-King shouted to a young giant. "Hugi! Come here. Come and race against Rapid."

Rapid and Hugi eyed each other up.

"Now," said the Giant-King. "This field is one mile long and you must run from one end to the other. There's a white marker post at the half-way point."

Rapid and Hugi made their way to the starting post. Then the Giant-King lifted up his right hand and, as soon as he dropped it, the race began.

Rapid was as fast as a hare, he was as fleet as a deer, but he wasn't as quick as the young giant. Hugi got to the far end of the field long before Rapid, and even had time to turn round and greet him.

"You're going to have to try harder," the Giant-King told Rapid. "Still, I must admit that I've never seen any man on Middle Earth run faster."

"I told you," Ristil piped up.

Rapid and Hugi made their way back to the starting post. "Go on," Ristil told her brother. "You can beat him. I think he's tricking you." But at the end of the second race, Rapid was as far behind Hugi as the distance you can shoot an arrow with a crossbow.

"Your brother is fast," the Giant-King told Ristil. "But he's no match for Hugi. Let's

watch them run one more race, and then we'll know for sure."

Rapid and Hugi walked back to the starting post for a third time. Rapid's legs hurt. His feet hurt. And he saw how Hugi was still so full of energy that his feet hardly touched the shaggy grass.

"Ready?" roared the Giant-King. "Steady? Run!"

Ristil and Thor and Loki cheered Rapid on, but it was no good. In fact, it was much worse than before. Rapid hadn't even got to the white marker post before Hugi had reached the far end of the paddock. Ristil sprinted towards her brother and Loki gave Thor a look. "I warned you," he said.

"That's that," said the Giant-King. "We can all see who the winner is. Now, Thor, what about you? Which one of your skills are you going to show us?"

Chapter 6
A Drop to Drink

"Me!" growled Thor. "Drinking."

"Drinking," the Giant-King said.

"You heard me. I'm thirsty. You haven't offered me a single drop to drink since we stepped into your hall."

"Very well," said the Giant-King.

"Yes. I'll have you know I can sink gallons and gallons, I can empty barrels of ale and never ever get drunk. I can drink more than any of the gods in my kingdom, Asgard."

The Giant-King led his four guests and all the ambling, shambling giants back into the hall, and there a servant put a drinking-horn between Thor's hands. It was brimming with golden ale.

Thor smiled. "Well, it's a big drinking horn," he admitted, "but I've seen bigger. It's an odd shape, though. A bit on the long side."

"Now, then," said the Giant-King. "We say that giants who can empty all the ale in one go are good drinkers. Some of us need two goes. But there's not a single giant in this fortress, male or female, old or young, who needs more than three goes."

Thor looked down into the horn. He saw his own reflection swimming in the ale, looking up at him. He raised the horn to his mouth and opened his throat. He tipped ale down it. Gallons and gallons. A whole tide. But the god ran out of breath before the horn was empty.

Thor burped. He burped again. Then he looked into the horn once more. He was shocked to see how much ale there was. The horn was still almost full.

"Thor," said the Giant-King in a puzzled voice. He sounded almost sorry. "Is that really the best you can do?"

Thor grabbed the horn again.

"You're just teasing us," the Giant-King said.

Thor lifted the horn. He gulped down the golden ale until he was gasping for breath. But he still couldn't finish it.

The Giant-King sniffed and swallowed his snot. "What's up?" he asked. "Newborn giants can drink more of their mother's milk than you've drunk from this horn."

Loki's eyes flickered. He liked the way the Giant-King taunted Thor.

"Now I understand," the Giant-King said. "A champion in Asgard is a chump in my kingdom."

"You can't say that," Ristil shouted.

"A winner in Asgard," sneered the Giant-King, "is a loser in my fortress."

Thor was furious. He jerked up the horn so that golden ale splashed all over his face and into his red beard. He sucked his cheeks. Then he swigged down more ale. He gulped and he gurgled, but he still couldn't empty the horn.

"More!" yelled the giants. "More, Thor!"

Thor held the long horn as far away from him as he could. He shoved it into the servant's hands.

The Giant-King looked down his nose. "Oh, dear!" he said. "Your fancy words, your bragging, they're all hot air. Brag-brag! Brag-brag! You're no drinker."

"I am," said Thor in a thick, gruff voice. "I've just drunk enough ale to drown every god in Asgard."

"What else can you do?" asked the Giant-King. "Is there any other skill you can show us?"

Chapter 7
Lifting and Wrestling

The Giant-King looked Thor the thunder-god up and down, and tut-tutted. "What am I to do with you? I can see you're no drinker and you're nothing like as strong as I thought …" He hummed and hawed. "Well," he said at last, "it's not much of a skill, but now and then some of the young giants do have a bit of fun picking up my cat."

"Your cat!" spat Thor.

Loki and Rapid laughed. Even Ristil laughed.

The Giant-King gave a sigh, and smiled. "Yes," he said. "Well ..." Then he patted his chair with his right hand, and under his big chair, a grey cat stirred. It uncurled itself. It uncoiled itself.

Thor took one step towards the cat, pushed an arm under it, and pulled. The grey cat simply blinked and arched its back.

Thor grunted. He bent down, linked both hands under the cat, and heaved. Again the cat arched its back until it looked like a grey, furry rainbow. But its four paws were still firmly planted on the ground.

"Come on!" said the Giant-King. "Try harder, Thor!"

Loki shook his head. "Since when was hard work any match for magic?" he murmured.

Now Thor crouched right under the cat. He reached up. He pushed with both hands. He jabbed his ten finger-tips into the cat's belly.

The grey cat gave a cough and lifted one front paw.

"That's enough, Thor," the Giant-King said. "The truth is, you're a midget, and your boasts are nothing but blither-blather."

Then Thor, the thunder-god, roared. The great hall shook, and the wooden platters rattled on the long tables.

"Does anyone here dare to wrestle with me?" shouted Thor. "Anyone at all?"

The Giant-King looked around the hall. "Dare," he said. His little smile made Thor shake with anger. "Dare to wrestle with you? No one here thinks you're worth bothering with."

Thor was mad with anger. He grabbed the handle of his hammer.

"I know!" said the Giant-King. And he turned to one of his servants. "Go and find Elli. Tell her to come to the hall."

All round the benches, the giants chuckled and gurgled, and rocked to and fro, and spat saliva on to the rush-floor.

"You can wrestle with Elli, my old foster-mother," the Giant-King told Thor. "She's flattened many a man much stronger than you are."

A wizened, bent old giantess came hobbling into the hall.

"Mother," said the Giant-King, "will you take to the floor with my guest, Thor?"

"Take to the floor?" croaked Elli. "Me? Dance with the thunder-god?"

"Dance!" shouted the Giant-King. "No. Wrestle! Will you wrestle with Thor?"

Elli threw away her stick. It clattered off one of the stone walls, and a young giant caught it.

Thor was in no mood for waiting. At once he grabbed hold of both of Elli's arms. But the moment he did so he knew she was far, far stronger than she looked. Her bony arms felt as if they were made of metal.

Thor tried to lift the old giantess. He put both his arms around her and tried to squeeze the breath out of her. He tried to rock her from side to side, and throw her off balance.

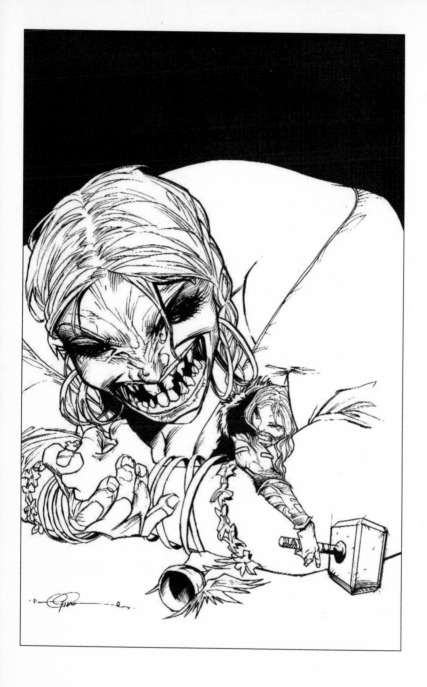

"Down and out!" shouted Rapid.

"Thor!" yelled Ristil, "Show her! Throw her!"

Suddenly the old crone spun round so that her back was towards Thor. She lifted her right arm and caught the god in a headlock. Then she dragged him round the hall. All the watching giants bellowed and cheered.

Now the horrible old giantess grinned so everyone could see her teeth. They were black and green. She squeezed Thor's neck. She pressed him, she crushed him, she forced him down, down until he had to drop on to one knee.

"Enough!" bawled the Giant-King. "We can see how well Thor wrestles. We've all seen plenty of his skills."

Thor stood up. He did not look Elli in the eye.

"What with running and eating and drinking and wrestling, it's getting late," the Giant-King told Thor and his friends. "You're all welcome to sleep in my hall tonight."

So the giants made room for Thor and Loki and Rapid and Ristil on their benches, and they treated them like important guests. Servants brought them big platters of sizzling meat (but not to Loki) and horns brimming with golden ale (but not to Thor). They laid out bedding and soft pillows.

Thor and his companions lay around the fire in the places that were kept for important visitors. They stretched out. They yawned. Very soon, they fell sound asleep.

Chapter 8
Master of Magic

Early next morning, the Giant-King himself led Thor and his friends out of the Great Hall. He walked with them across the sandy plain.

Thor and Loki were silent. They were thinking about everything that had happened. But Rapid and Ristil were as bright and breezy as early birds now that they had got out of the fortress and were safe. They chattered and laughed, and several times they began to sing.

"I'll let you go now," the Giant-King told the four travellers. "But first, let me ask you – are you glad you came to my fortress?"

"No!" growled Thor.

"Was everything as you expected?"

"Nothing," Thor replied. "You've made a fool of me and I've come off second best. What's more, you'll tell everyone about it."

The Giant-King stopped and stared at Thor. He pointed at him with his right forefinger – it was as long and thick as a rolling-pin.

"I'll tell you this," he rasped. "I'm going to make quite sure you never, never see the inside of my fortress again."

Thor frowned.

"I'd never have let you in if I'd known how strong you are."

"Second best," Thor mumbled. "You showed me up. And now you're mocking me."

"Listen!" said the Giant-King. "Do you remember that bag, the one you couldn't unstrap?"

"Big Bloke's bag," said Loki.

"I did up those straps," the Giant-King told them.

Thor looked puzzled.

"Big Bloke – that was me," the Giant-King went on. "Can you see that hill that looks like a saddle, the one with those three valleys? Thor, you made those valleys. You made three valleys when you walloped me. I put that hill between us ..."

Thor gazed at the Giant-King. How could this be?

"I made the hill with magic spells. To save my life," the Giant-King told Thor. Then he turned to Loki. "In my hall, you ate fast. Extremely fast. But you couldn't beat that young giant I set against you. He is Wildfire itself. That's why he was able to eat up all the bones and the wooden table as well."

Ristil grinned from ear to ear. "You tricked the Trickster!" she said.

Loki smiled a slow twisted smile. "Magic," he murmured. "The Giant-King is a master of magic."

Ristil looked up at the Giant-King. "What about my brother?" she demanded. "I think you tricked him too."

"I did," said the Giant-King. "Rapid ran three races against Hugi, and Hugi is my own Thought. My own thinking. Rapid ran fast all right, extremely fast, but not even he can keep up with the speed of Thought."

Ristil gave her brother a poke in the ribs. "Told you," she said in a loud whisper.

"As for you, Thor," the Giant-King went on, "you said that drinking horn looked a bit on the long side. It was! The pointy end stretched right down into the sea. When you're by the sea, have a careful look. It's much lower now than it was before.

"And my grey cat," said the Giant-King, "he's the great snake that lies at the bottom of the sea. He's the snake that lies right round Middle Earth, with his own tail in his mouth. Thor, you pushed up his back so that it pressed against the sky."

The Giant-King slowly shook his head. "My foster-mother, Elli, is Old Age. Thor, you wrestled with Old Age. How you wrestled! She couldn't throw you. She was only able to force you down on to one knee. I've been making magic to trick you and tame you all along."

For a moment, short as a breath and long as forever, the Giant-King and Thor and Loki and the farmer's two children stood together without saying a word. Thor kept clenching and unclenching his fists, and the Giant-King stared at the thunder-god. They'd slept by the same fire, in the same hall, but they were still deadly enemies.

"You're very strong," said the Giant-King, "but I've made magic to guard my fortress and I'll make it again. However strong you are, and however hard you try, you'll never be able to harm me."

Thor grabbed his great hammer with both hands. He roared and swung it over his head. He shut his eyes and so did his friends. Then they opened them again ...

The Giant-King had vanished.

Rapid and Ristil gasped.

Loki just laughed.

Thor began to run back towards the grim walls of the fortress, the gates, the high halls, the cheering, sneering, jeering giants. But there were no walls. No gates. Nothing. Nothing but a bone-cold wind coming right off the mountains. Nothing but a sandy, shimmering plain.

BATTLE CARDS

Kevin Crossley-Holland

Author

Favourite hero:
Beowulf. Not only is he a superman who fights two monsters and a dragon but he's kind and fair and loyal.

Favourite monster:
The Slithergadee - revolting and indescribable, who crawled out of the sea and catches everyone and everything.

Your weapon of choice:
A spiked mace.

Favourite fight scene:
The battle between the giants and the monsters at the end of the Norse myth makes my blood race.

Goodie or baddie:
Goodie. At first it seems great to be a baddie, but it's foul.

RELOADED

WHO WILL WIN?

Siku

Illustrator

Favourite hero:
Batman – who else? Batman is for grown-ups, Spiderman is for kids and Superman is just a loser who wears red pants outside his blue suit ... give me a break!

Favourite monster:
Everyone loves King Kong – besides, he isn't slimy.

Your weapon of choice:
Telekinesis - moving things with my mind.

Favourite fight scene:
When Bruce Lee faces Chuck Norris in the film Way of the Dragon.

Goodie or baddie:
A goodie scaring the life out of bad bosses.

RELOADED

Barrington Stoke would like to thank all its readers for commenting on the manuscript before publication and in particular:

Kieron Amyes
Kelly Bennetts
Louisa Bryant
Hannah Capewell
Lee Chaffe
Elliot Cook
Janey Cooper
Sam Cornick
Sarah Dunn
Nick Garratt
Adam Harber

Dillon Lefler
Megan Lines
Alwyn Martin
Joseph Martin
Lucy Maunsell
Luke Morris
Chris Symon
Ashley Walsh
Charlotte Webb
Susan Wheeler
Lizzy Wills

Become a Consultant!

Would you like to give us feedback on our titles before they are published? Contact us at the email address below – we'd love to hear from you!

info@barringtonstoke.co.uk
www.barringtonstoke.co.uk

MORE MONSTERS,
MORE MAGIC,
MORE MAYHEM ...

BIMA
AND THE
WATER OF LIFE

BY
FRANZESKA G. EWART

A hero who lives for danger
An adventure to the ends of the earth
An evil from the darkest nightmares
A battle that will go down in history ...
Bima and the Water of Life

You can order *Bima and the Water of Life* directly from
www.barringtonstoke.co.uk